This book belongs to

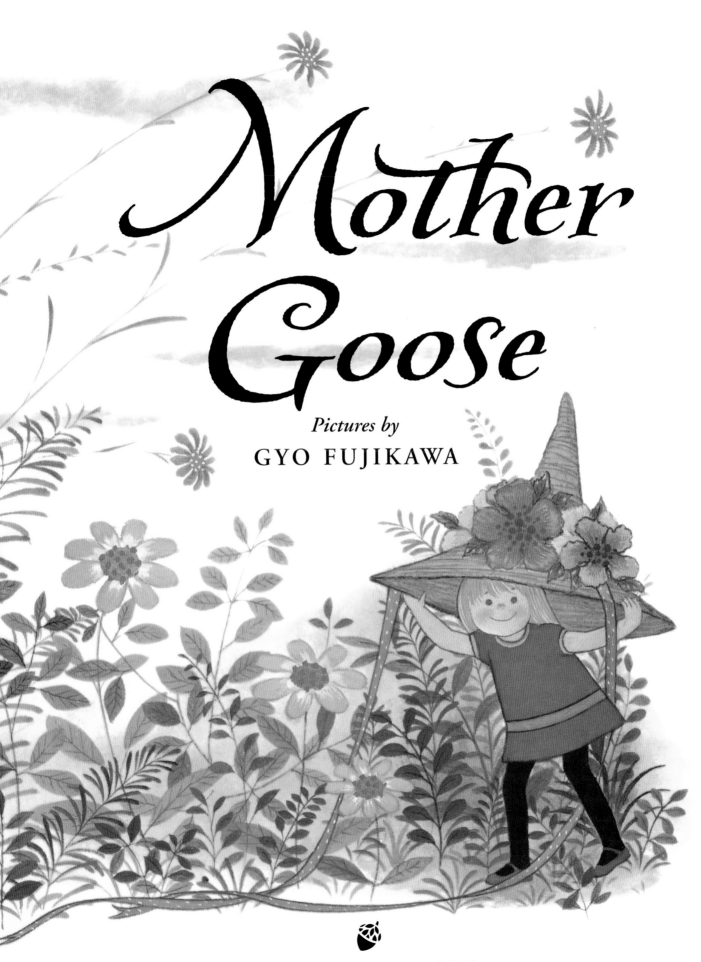

Mother Goose

Pictures by
GYO FUJIKAWA

STERLING CHILDREN'S BOOKS
New York

STERLING CHILDREN'S BOOKS
New York

An Imprint of Sterling Publishing
387 Park Avenue South
New York, NY 10016

ISBN 978-1-4027-5064-9

Distributed in Canada by Sterling Publishing
c/o Canadian Manda Group, 165 Dufferin Street
Toronto, Ontario, Canada M6K 3H6
Distributed in the United Kingdom by GMC Distribution Services
Castle Place, 166 High Street, Lewes, East Sussex, England BN7 1XU
Distributed in Australia by Capricorn Link (Australia) Pty. Ltd.
P.O. Box 704, Windsor, NSW 2756, Australia

For information about custom editions, special sales, premium and corporate purchases, please contact
Sterling Special Sales Department at 800-805-5489 or specialsales@sterlingpublishing.com.

Manufactured in China
Lot #:
13
07/16

www.sterlingpublishing.com/kids

Contents

	Page
Old Mother Goose	15
The Owl	17
Mary Had a Pretty Bird	17
A Needle and a Thread	17
Ding, Dong, Bell	17
Under a Hill	18
A Busy Day	19
Haymaking	19
Merry are the Bells	20
Banbury Fair	20
Pussy-Cat Mew	20
Two Comical Folk	21
A Cherry	21
Pat-a-Cake	21
Simple Simon	22
The Hart	22
To the Snow	22
The Cat and the Fiddle	23
Barber, Barber	23
Tally-Ho!	23
Going to Bed	23
What's in There?	24
Cock-a-doodle-do!	24
Two Little Dicky Birds	24
At Brill	25
The Lion and the Unicorn	25
The Little Mouse	25
Patience is a Virtue	25
Rock-a-Bye, Baby	26
March Winds	27
The Balloon	28
The Girl in the Lane	28
Pussy Cat	28
Sally	28
The Clever Hen	28
Cock-Crow	29
Daddy	29
Porringer	29
Jack-a-Nory	29
Coffee and Tea	29
The Old Woman of Gloucester	29
The Alphabet	30
Queen Anne	32
Solomon Grundy	32
Nothing	32
Rain	32
Jack Sprat	33
The Crooked Sixpence	33
Jeremiah	33
Cantaloupes	33
The Gossips	33

	Page
I Saw Three Ships	34
Little Ships	35
Jack and His Fiddle	36
Elsie Marley	36
Ipsey Wipsey	36
Pease Porridge Hot	36
To the Bat	37
An Old Woman	37
Boys and Girls	37
Pussy-Cat, Where Have You Been?	37
The Robins	38
Bobby Shaftoe	38
Ducks and Drakes	38
Jack and Jill	39
Hannah Bantry	40
One, Two, Three, Four, Five	40
Punch and Judy	40
Needles and Pins	40
The Merchants of London	41
Play Days	41
There Was a Rat	41
Little Tom Tucker	41
Old King Cole	42
Red Sky	43
Baa, Baa, Black Sheep	43
Sing, Sing	43
The Bachelor's Lament	44
Old Farmer Giles	44
Cobbler, Cobbler	44
Mrs. Mason's Basin	45
Whistle	45
Bees	45
London Bridge	46
Jacky Jingle	46
Will You Lend Me?	46
Cock Robin Got Up Early	47
Three Men in a Tub	47
Bow-Wow	47
St. Swithin's Day	48
For Want of a Nail	48
Green Gravel	48
Bagpipes	48
Pit, Pat	49
Three Young Rats	49
A Sunshiny Shower	50
When it Rains	50
Little Sally Waters	50
Doctor Foster	50
One Misty, Moisty Morning	51
Two Pigeons	52
The Mischievous Raven	52

	Page
Blow, Wind, Blow	53
Dibbity, Dibbity	53
The Black Hen	53
This is the Way	53
Sing a Song of Sixpence	54
Purple Plums	55
Diddlety, Diddlety, Dumpty	55
Queen Caroline	56
This Little Man Lived All Alone	56
Shall We Go A-Shearing?	56
Three Ghostesses	56
Bye, Baby Bunting	56
The Man in Our Town	57
It's Raining	57
Cross-Patch	57
Birds of a Feather	57
Higglety, Pigglety	57
Fears and Tears	57
I Saw a Ship a-Sailing	59
Moses	60
Dickory, Dickory, Dare	60
The Rugged Rock	60
Little Miss	60
Fiddle-de-dee	60
Sulky Sue	60
The Little Boy	60
The First of May	61
Jenny	61
At Belle Isle	61
To Babylon	61
Cakes and Custard	61
Green Cheese	61
Jerry Hall	61
The Mulberry Bush	62
John Watts	62
One, Two, Buckle My Shoe	63
Hot Boiled Beans	63
Caution	63
What Can the Matter Be?	64
Wines and Cakes	64
Doctor Fell	64
The King of France	65
A Dog and a Cat	65
Bryan O'Lin	65
The Church and the Steeple	65
The Old Woman in a Shoe	66
The Man Who Had Naught	68
There Was a Little Girl	68
Diddle, Diddle, Dumpling	68
Multiplication is Vexation	68
Mother Shuttle	69

	Page
The Milkmaid	69
Poor Dog Bright	69
The Robin	70
Tom, Tom, the Piper's Son	70
Harvest	70
Ring-a-Ring o' Roses	71
Hoddley, Poddley	71
Hush, Little Baby	71
Elizabeth	72
The Man in the Wilderness	72
Days in the Month	72
Poll Parrot	72
Two Little Dogs	72
Saturday Night	73
See-saw, Sacradown	73
Wibbleton and Wobbleton	73
Candle Saving	73
Going to St. Ives	73
The Moon	74
The Star	75
Girls and Boys, Come Out to Play	75
Ten Little Bluebirds	76
The House that Jack Built	78
Race Starting	80
Hot Cross Buns	80
The Greedy Man	80
That's All	80
Pussy Sits Beside the Fire	81
To the Ladybird	81
Tommy Trot	81
My Little Dog	81
Little Maiden	81
Good Night	81
Little Bo-Peep	82
Daffodils	82
Niddle-Noddle	83
The Queen of Hearts	84
Nothing-at-All	84
Davy Dumpling	84
Pins	84
The Wind	85
To Market, to Market	85
Taffy was a Welshman	85
The Milk Maid	86
Little Bird	86
Blind Man's Buff	86
Hickory, Dickory, Dock	87
Lavender's Blue	87
This Litle Pig	87
This Old Man	88
Gregory Griggs	88
Fire! Fire!	88
Banbury Cross	89
The Jolly Miller	89
A Nick and a Nock	89

	Page
Magic Words	89
Three Wise Men of Gotham	91
If	91
Little King Pippin	92
See-Saw, Margery Daw	92
Man of Derby	92
Pairs or Pears	93
The Key of the Kingdom	93
I Had a Little Moppet	93
Terence McDiddler	93
Old Chairs to Mend	94
Hector Protector	94
I Sing, I Sing	94
Yankee Doodle	94
Little Fishes	95
Little Betty Blue	95
Six Little Mice	95
Dame Trot	96
Poor Old Robinson Crusoe	96
The Ten O'Clock Scholar	96
I Had a Little Nut Tree	97
Burnie Bee	97
Hark! Hark!	97
Lazy Mary	97
Robin Redbreast	98
Little Miss Muffet	98
Mary, Mary, Quite Contrary	99
Come Hither	100
Lucy Locket	100
There was an Owl	101
The Donkey	101
John Fought for His Beloved Land	101
Anna Maria	101
Wash the Dishes	101
Old Mother Hubbard	102
Mary Had a Little Lamb	103
The Pumpkin Eater	103
The Muffin Man	104
Peter White's Nose	104
Georgie Porgie	104
Betty Botter's Butter	104
Hob, Shoe, Hob	104
A Week of Birthdays	105
Goose Feathers	105
Run, Boys, Run	105
Hobbledy Hops	105
As I Was Going Along	105
Old Woman, Old Woman	106
Wee Willie Winkie	106
Star Light	107
Bedtime	107
A Candle	107
The Mist	107
Kindness	108
Handy Dandy	108

	Page
Come Tie My Cravat	108
A Chimney	108
Shoe a Little Horse	108
I Love Sixpence	109
The Bad Rider	109
If All the World	109
Great A, Little a	109
Three Little Kittens	110
Curly-Locks	111
Humpty Dumpty	111
Jumping Joan	111
Two Little Blackbirds	111
Friday Night's Dream	111
The Spider and the Fly	112
Sneeze on Monday	112
I Had a Little Husband	112
The Clock	113
If Wishes Were Horses	113
Jack, Be Nimble	113
The Teeth	113
Little Boy Blue	114
Bob Robin	115
Tommy Tittlemouse	115
Goosey, Goosey, Gander	116
Hey, My Kitten	116
Polly Flinders	116
Leg Over Leg	116
Billy Boy	117
My Maid Mary	117
Handy Pandy	117
There Was a Bee	117
Rain	118
Lengthening Days	118
Little Jack Horner	119
Tommy and Bessy	119
Little Blue Ben	119
Tweedledum and Tweedledee	120
The Hobby Horse	120
All Work and No Play	120
Three Blind Mice	120
Pop Goes the Weasel	121
The Kilkenny Cats	121
Tea Time	121
Little Jack Pumpkin Face	121
Bow-Wow-Wow!	122
The Owl	123
By Myself	123
Ride Away, Ride Away	124
The Cuckoo	124
Little Girl	124
Hay is for Horses	124
For Every Evil	124
Do You Love Me?	125
Christmas is Coming	125
Bedtime	125
And Now, Good Night	125

Mother Goose

Old Mother Goose

Old Mother Goose,
When she wanted to wander,
Would ride through the air
On a very fine gander.

She lived in a house
That was built in a wood
Where an owl at the door
For a sentinel stood.

She had a son, Jack,
A plain-looking lad;
He was not very good,
Nor yet very bad.

She sent him to market —
A live goose he bought.
"Here, Mother," says he,
"It will not go for naught."

Jack's goose and her gander
Grew very fond;
They'd both eat together,
Or swim in the pond.

Jack found one fine morning,
As I have been told,
His goose had laid him
An egg of pure gold.

Jack ran to his mother,
The news for to tell;
She called him a good boy
And said it was well.

Jack sold his gold egg
To a rascally knave.
Not half of its value
To poor Jack he gave.

And then the gold egg
Was thrown into the sea,
When Jack he jumped in
And got it back presently.

Then Jack went a-courting
A lady so gay,
As fair as the lily,
And sweet as the May.

The knave got the goose,
Which he vowed he would kill,
Resolving at once
His pockets to fill.

The knave and the squire
Came up at his back,
And began to belabor
The sides of poor Jack.

Jack's mother came in
And caught the goose soon,
And mounting its back,
Flew up to the moon.

16

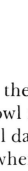

The Owl

Of all the gay birds that e'er I did see,
The owl is the fairest by far to me,
For all day long she sits in a tree,
And when the night comes, away flies she.

Mary Had a Pretty Bird

Mary had a pretty bird,
    Feathers bright and yellow;
Slender legs, upon my word,
    He was a pretty fellow.

The sweetest notes he always sang,
    Which much delighted Mary;
And near the cage she'd ever sit,
    To hear her own canary.

A Needle and a Thread

Old Mother Twitchett had but one eye,
And a long tail, which she let fly;
And every time she went over a gap,
A bit of her tail she left in a trap.

Ding, Dong, Bell

Ding, dong, bell,
Pussy's in the well.
Who put her in?
Little Johnny Green.
Who pulled her out?
Little Johnny Stout.
What a naughty boy was that
To try to drown poor pussy cat,
Who never did him any harm,
But killed the mice in his father's barn.

Under a Hill

There was an old woman
    Lived under a hill,
And if she's not gone,
    She lives there still.

Baked apples she sold,
    And cranberry pies,
And she's the old woman
    Who never told lies.

18

A Busy Day

The cock's on the housetop,
    Blowing his horn,
The men are in the barn,
    Threshing the corn,
The maids are in the meadow,
    Making the hay,
The ducks are in the river,
    Swimming away.

Haymaking

Willy boy, Willy boy, where are you going?
I will go with you if that I may.
I'm going to the meadow to see them a-mowing,
I am going to help them to make the new hay.

Merry are the Bells

Merry are the bells and merry would they ring,
Merry was myself, and merry could I sing;
With a merry ding-dong, happy, gay, and free,
And a merry sing-song, happy let us be!

Waddle goes your gait, and hollow are your hose,
Noddle goes your pate, and purple is your nose;
Merry is your sing-song, happy, gay, and free,
With a merry ding-dong, happy let us be!

Merry have we met, and merry have we been,
Merry let us part, and merry meet again;
With our merry sing-song, happy, gay, and free,
And a merry ding-dong, happy let us be!

Banbury Fair

As I was going to Banbury,
    Upon a summer's day,
My dame had butter, eggs and fruit,
    And I had corn and hay.
Joe drove the ox, and Tom the swine,
    Dick took the foal and mare;
I sold them all — then home to dine,
    From famous Banbury fair.

Pussy-Cat Mew

Pussy-Cat Mew jumped over a coal
And in her best petticoat burned a great hole.
Poor pussy's weeping, she'll have no more milk
Until her best petticoat's mended with silk.

Two Comical Folk

In a cottage in Fife
Lived a man and his wife,
Who, believe me, were comical folk;
For, to people's surprise,
They both saw with their eyes,
And their tongues moved whenever they spoke.
When quite fast asleep,
I've been told that to keep
Their eyes open they could not contrive;
They walked on their feet,
And 'twas thought what they eat
Helped, with drinking, to keep them alive.

Penny and Penny

Penny and penny,
Laid up will be many;
Who will not save a penny
Shall never have any.

A Cherry

As I went through the garden gap,
Who should I meet but Dick Redcap!
A stick in his hand, a stone in his throat,
If you'll tell me this riddle, I'll give you a groat.

Pat-a-Cake

Pat-a-cake, pat-a-cake, baker's man,
Bake me a cake as fast as you can.
Pat it and prick it and mark it with T,
And put it in the oven for Tommy and me.

Simple Simon

Simple Simon met a pieman
    Going to the fair;
Says Simple Simon to the pieman,
    "Let me taste your ware."

Says the pieman to Simple Simon,
    "Show me first your penny."
Says Simple Simon to the pieman,
    "Indeed, I have not any."

Simple Simon went a-fishing,
    For to catch a whale;
All the water he had got
    Was in his mother's pail.

He went to catch a dickey bird
    And thought he could not fail,
Because he'd got a little salt
    To put upon its tail.

He went to shoot a wild duck,
    But wild duck flew away;
Says Simon, "I can't hit him,
    Because he will not stay."

The Hart

The hart he loves the high wood,
    The hare she loves the hill;
The knight he loves his bright sword,
    The lady loves her will.

To the Snow

Snow, snow faster,
Ally-ally-blaster;
The old woman's plucking her geese,
Selling the feathers a penny a piece.

The Cat and the Fiddle

Hey, diddle, diddle, the cat and the fiddle,
    The cow jumped over the moon;
The little dog laughed to see such sport,
    And the dish ran away with the spoon.

Barber, Barber

Barber, barber, shave a pig,
How many hairs will make a wig?
Four and twenty, that's enough.
Give the barber a pinch of snuff.

Tally-Ho!

Tally-Ho! Tally-Ho!
A-hunting we will go!
We'll catch a fox
And put him in a box
And never let him go.

Going to Bed

Go to bed late,
Stay very small;
Go to bed early,
Grow very tall.

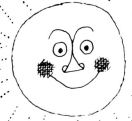

What's In There?

What's in there?
Gold and money.
Where's my share?
The mousie's run away with it.
Where's the mousie?
In her housie.
Where's her housie?
In the wood.
Where's the wood?
The fire burned it.
Where's the fire?
The water quenched it.
Where's the water?
The brown bull drank it.
Where's the brown bull?
Behind Burnie's hill.
Where's Burnie's hill?
All dressed in snow.
Where's the snow?
The sun melted it.
Where's the sun?
High, high up in the air.

Cock-a-doodle-do!

Cock-a-doodle-do!
My dame has lost her shoe,
My master's lost his fiddlestick,
And knows not what to do.

Cock-a-doodle-do!
What is my dame to do?
Till master finds his fiddlestick,
She'll dance without her shoe.

Two Little Dicky Birds

Two little dicky birds,
Sitting on a wall;
One named Peter,
The other named Paul.
Fly away, Peter!
Fly away, Paul!
Come back, Peter!
Come back, Paul!

At Brill

At Brill on the hill
The wind blows shrill,
The cook no meat can dress;
At Stow-on-the-Wold
The wind blows cold,
I know no more than this.

The Lion and the Unicorn

The lion and the unicorn
   Were fighting for the crown;
The lion beat the unicorn
   All around the town.

Some gave them white bread,
   And some gave them brown;
Some gave them plum cake
   And drummed them out of town.

The Little Mouse

I have seen you, little mouse,
Running all about the house,
Through the hole your little eye
In the wainscot peeping sly,
Hoping soon some crumbs to steal
To make quite a hearty meal.
Look before you venture out,
See if pussy is about.
If she's gone, you'll quickly run
To the larder for some fun;
Round about the dishes creep,
Taking into each a peep
To choose the daintiest that's there,
Spoiling things you do not care.

Patience is a Virtue

Patience is a virtue,
   Virtue is a grace;
Both put together
   Make a very pretty face.

25

Rock-a-Bye, Baby

Rock-a-bye, baby, on the tree top;
When the wind blows, the cradle will rock;
When the bough breaks, the cradle will fall;
Down will come baby, cradle and all.

March Winds

March winds and April showers
Bring forth May flowers.

The Balloon

"What's the news of the day,
Good neighbor, I pray?"
"They say the balloon
Has gone up to the moon."

The Girl in the Lane

The girl in the lane that couldn't speak plain
Cried, "Gobble, gobble, gobble."
The man on the hill that couldn't stand still
Went hobble, hobble, hobble.

Pussy Cat

Pussy Cat ate the dumplings!
Pussy Cat ate the dumplings!
  Mamma stood by
  And cried, "Oh, fie!
WHY did you eat the dumplings?"

The Clever Hen

I had a little hen,
    The prettiest ever seen;
She washed me the dishes
    And kept the house clean.
She went to the mill
    To fetch me some flour;
She brought it home in
    Less than an hour.
She baked me my bread,
    She brewed me my ale,
She sat by the fire
    And told many a fine tale.

Sally

Sally go round the sun,
Sally go round the moon,
Sally go round the chimney pots
On a Saturday afternoon.

Cock-Crow

Cocks crow in the morn to tell us to rise,
And he who lies late will never be wise.
For early to bed and early to rise
Makes a man healthy, wealthy and wise.

Daddy

Bring Daddy home
    With a fiddle and a drum,
A pocket full of spices,
    An apple and a plum.

Porringer

What is the rhyme for porringer?
The King he had a daughter fair,
And gave the Prince of Orange her!

Jack-a-Nory

I'll tell you a story
  About Jack-a-Nory,
And now my story's begun.
I'll tell you another
  Of Jack and his brother,
And now my story is done.

Coffee and Tea

Molly, my sister, and I fell out,
And what do you think it was all about?
She loved coffee and I loved tea,
And that was the reason we couldn't agree.

The Old Woman of Gloucester

There was an old woman of Gloucester,
Whose parrot two guineas it cost here,
  But its tongue, never ceasing,
  Was vastly displeasing
To the talkative woman of Gloucester.

THE ALPHABET

A B C

I J K L M

S T U V W

Queen Anne

Lady Queen Anne she sits in the sun,
As fair as a lily, as white as a swan;
Come taste my lily, come smell my rose,
Which of my maidens do you choose?
The ball is ours and none of yours,
Go to the wood and gather flowers.
Cats and kittens now stay within,
While we young maidens walk out and in.

Solomon Grundy

Solomon Grundy,
Born on a Monday,
Christened on Tuesday,
Married on Wednesday,
Took ill on Thursday,
Worse on Friday,
Died on Saturday,
Buried on Sunday.
This is the end
Of Solomon Grundy.

Nothing

There was an old woman
    And nothing she had,
And so this old woman
    Was said to be mad.
She'd nothing to eat,
    She'd nothing to wear,
She'd nothing to lose,
    She'd nothing to fear,
She'd nothing to ask,
    And nothing to give,
And when she did die,
    She'd nothing to leave.

Rain

Rain, rain, go away,
Come again another day,
Little Johnny wants to play.
Rain, rain, go to Spain,
Never show your face again.

Jack Sprat

Jack Sprat could eat no fat,
His wife could eat no lean;
And so, betwixt them both, you see,
They licked the platter clean.

The Crooked Sixpence

There was a crooked man
    And he went a crooked mile;
He found a crooked sixpence
    Beside a crooked stile;
He bought a crooked cat
    Which caught a crooked mouse,
And they all lived together
    In a little crooked house.

Jeremiah

Jeremiah, blow the fire,
    Puff, puff, puff!
First you blow it gently,
    Then you blow it rough.

Cantaloupes

Cantaloupes! Cantaloupes!
What is the price?
Eight for a dollar,
And all very nice.

The Gossips

Miss One, Two and Three
    Could never agree
While they gossiped around
    A tea-caddy.

33

I Saw Three Ships

I saw three ships come sailing by,
Come sailing by, come sailing by,
I saw three ships come sailing by,
On New Year's Day in the morning.

And what do you think was in them then?
Was in them then, was in them then?
And what do you think was in them then,
On New Year's Day in the morning?

Three pretty girls were in them then,
Were in them then, were in them then,
Three pretty girls were in them then,
On New Year's Day in the morning.

And one could whistle, and one could sing,
And one could play on the violin;
Such joy there was at my wedding,
On New Year's Day in the morning.

Little Ships

Little ships must keep the shore;
Larger ships may venture more.

Jack and His Fiddle

"Jacky, come and give me thy fiddle,
　　If ever thou mean to thrive."
"Nay, I'll not give any fiddle
　　To any man alive.
If I should give my fiddle,
　　They'll think that I've gone mad;
For many a joyous day
　　My fiddle and I have had."

Elsie Marley

Elsie Marley is grown so fine,
She won't get up to feed the swine,
But lies in bed till eight or nine.
　　Lazy Elsie Marley.

Ipsey Wipsey

Ipsey Wipsey spider
　　Climbing up the spout;
Down came the rain
　　And washed the spider out;
Out came the sunshine
　　And dried up all the rain;
Ipsey Wipsey spider
　　Climbing up again.

Pease Porridge Hot

Pease porridge hot,
　　Pease porridge cold,
Pease porridge in the pot,
　　Nine days old.
Some like it hot,
　　Some like it cold,
Some like it in the pot,
　　Nine days old.

To the Bat

Bat, bat, come under my hat,
　　And I'll give you a slice of bacon;
And when I bake, I'll give you a cake,
　　If I am not mistaken.

An Old Woman

There was an old woman, and what do you think?
She lived upon nothing but victuals and drink.
Victuals and drink were the chief of her diet,
And yet this old woman could never keep quiet.

Boys and Girls

What are little boys made of, made of?
What are little boys made of?
　　Snips and snails,
　　And puppy dogs' tails,
That's what little boys are made of.

What are little girls made of, made of?
What are little girls made of?
　　Sugar and spice
　　And all that's nice,
That's what little girls are made of.

Pussy-Cat, Where Have You Been?

"Pussy-Cat, Pussy-Cat, where have you been?"
"I've been to London to visit the Queen."
"Pussy-Cat, Pussy-Cat, what did you there?"
"I frightened a little mouse under the chair."

The Robins

A robin and a robin's son
Once went to town to buy a bun.
They couldn't decide on plum or plain,
And so they went back home again.

Bobby Shaftoe

Bobby Shaftoe's gone to sea,
Silver buckles on his knee;
He'll come back and marry me,
    Pretty Bobby Shaftoe!

Bobby Shaftoe's fat and fair
Combing down his yellow hair;
He's my love forevermore,
    Pretty Bobby Shaftoe!

Ducks and Drakes

A duck and a drake,
A nice barley cake,
With a penny to pay the old baker;
A hop and a scotch
Is another notch,
Slitherum, slatherum, take her.

38

Jack and Jill

Jack and Jill went up the hill
    To fetch a pail of water.
Jack fell down and broke his crown,
    And Jill came tumbling after.

Then up Jack got and home did trot,
    As fast as he could caper;
Went to bed to mend his head
    With vinegar and brown paper.

Hannah Bantry

Hannah Bantry, in the pantry,
Gnawing at a mutton bone;
How she gnawed it,
How she clawed it,
When she found herself alone.

One, Two, Three, Four, Five

One, two, three, four, five,
Once I caught a fish alive,
Six, seven, eight, nine, ten,
Then I let it go again.
Why did you let it go?
Because it bit my finger so.
Which finger did it bite?
The little finger on the right.

1, 2, 3, 4, 5,
6, 7, 8, 9, 10

Punch and Judy

Punch and Judy
   Fought for a pie;
Punch gave Judy
   A knock in the eye.
Says Punch to Judy,
   "Will you have any more?"
Says Judy to Punch,
   "My eye is sore."

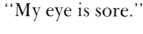

Needles and Pins

Needles and pins, needles and pins,
When a man marries, his trouble begins.

The Merchants of London

Hey diddle, dinketty, poppety, pet,
The merchants of London they wear scarlet;
Silk in the collar and gold in the hem,
So merrily march the merchant men.

Play Days

How many days has my baby to play?
Saturday, Sunday, Monday,
Tuesday, Wednesday, Thursday, Friday,
Saturday, Sunday, Monday.
Hop away, skip away,
My baby wants to play;
My baby wants to play every day.

There Was a Rat

There was a rat,
    For want of stairs,
Went down a rope
    To say his prayers.

Little Tom Tucker

Little Tom Tucker
    Sings for his supper.
What shall we give him?
    White bread and butter.
How shall he cut it
    Without any knife?
How shall he marry
    Without any wife?

Old King Cole

Old King Cole
Was a merry old soul,
And a merry old soul was he;
He called for his pipe
And he called for his bowl,
And he called for his fiddlers three.

Every fiddler
Had a fiddle,
And a very fine fiddle had he;
Oh, there's none so rare
As can compare
With King Cole and his fiddlers three.

Red Sky

Red sky at night,
Shepherd's delight;
Red sky in the morning,
Shepherd's warning.

Baa, Baa, Black Sheep

Baa, baa, black sheep,
  Have you any wool?
Yes, sir, yes, sir,
  Three bags full;
One for the master,
  And one for the dame,
And one for the little boy
  Who lives down the lane.

Sing, Sing

Sing, sing, what shall I sing?
The cat's run away with the pudding string!
Do, do, what shall I do?
The cat has bitten it quite in two.

43

The Bachelor's Lament

When I was a little boy,
    I lived by myself.
And all the bread and cheese I got
    I laid upon a shelf.

The rats and the mice
    They made such a strife,
I had to go to London town
    And get me a wife.

The streets were so broad
    And the lanes were so narrow,
I was forced to bring my wife home
    In a wheelbarrow.

The wheelbarrow broke
    And my wife had a fall,
Farewell, wheelbarrow,
    Little wife and all.

Old Farmer Giles

Old Farmer Giles,
    He went seven miles
With his faithful dog, Old Rover;
    And Old Farmer Giles,
    When he came to the stiles,
Took a run, and jumped clean over.

Cobbler, Cobbler

Cobbler, cobbler, mend my shoe,
Get it done by half past two,
Stitch it up and stitch it down,
Then I'll give you half-a-crown.

Mrs. Mason's Basin

Mrs. Mason bought a basin.
Mrs. Tyson said, "What a nice 'un!"
"What did it cost?" said Mrs. Frost.
"Half a crown," said Mrs. Brown.
"Did it, indeed?" said Mrs. Reed.
"It did for certain," said Mrs. Burton.
Then Mrs. Nix, up to her tricks,
Threw the basin on the bricks.

Whistle

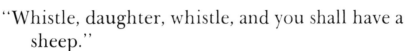

"Whistle, daughter, whistle, and you shall have a
    sheep."
"Mother, I cannot whistle; neither can I sleep."

"Whistle, daughter, whistle, and you shall have a
    cow."
"Mother, I cannot whistle; neither know I how."

"Whistle, daughter, whistle, and you shall have a
    man."
"Mother, I cannot whistle; but I'll do the best I can."

Bees

A swarm of bees in May
Is worth a load of hay;
A swarm of bees in June
Is worth a silver spoon;
A swarm of bees in July
Is not worth a fly.

London Bridge

London Bridge is falling down,
Falling down, falling down;
London Bridge is falling down,
My fair lady.

We must build it up again,
Up again, up again;
We must build it up again,
My fair lady.

Build it up with cotton thread,
Cotton thread, cotton thread;
Build it up with cotton thread,
My fair lady.

Cotton thread will not hold fast,
Not hold fast, not hold fast;
Cotton thread will not hold fast,
My fair lady.

Jacky Jingle

Now what do you think
Of little Jack Jingle?
Before he was married,
He used to live single.

But after he married,
To alter his life,
He left off living single
And lived with his wife.

Will You Lend Me ?

Will you lend me your mare to ride a mile?
No, she is lame leaping over a stile.
Alack! and I must go to the fair,
I'll give you good money for lending your mare.
Oh, oh! say you so?
Money will make the mare to go.

46

Cock Robin Got Up Early

Cock Robin got up early,
　　At the break of day,
And went to Jenny's window
　　To sing a roundelay.

He sang Cock Robin's love
　　To pretty Jenny Wren,
And when he got unto the end,
　　Then he began again.

Three Men in a Tub

Rub-a-dub-dub,
Three men in a tub,
And who do you think they be?
The butcher, the baker,
The candlestick maker,
They all jumped out of a rotten potato;
Turn 'em out, knaves all three!

Bow-Wow

Bow-wow says the dog,
　　Mew, mew says the cat,
Grunt, grunt goes the hog,
　　And squeak goes the rat.

Whoo-oo says the owl,
　　Caw, caw says the crow,
Quack, quack says the duck,
　　And what cuckoos say, you know.

So with cuckoos and owls,
　　With rats and with dogs,
With ducks and with crows,
　　With cats and with hogs,

A fine song I have made,
　　To please you, my dear;
And if it's well-sung,
　　'Twill be charming to hear.

St. Swithin's Day

St. Swithin's Day, if thou dost rain,
For forty days it will remain;
St. Swithin's Day, if thou be fine,
For forty days the sun will shine.

For Want of a Nail

For want of a nail,
    The shoe was lost;
For want of a shoe,
    The horse was lost;
For want of a horse,
    The rider was lost;
For want of a rider,
    The battle was lost;
For want of a battle,
    The kingdom was lost;
And all for the want
    Of a horseshoe nail.

Green Gravel

Green gravel, green gravel,
    Until it grows green,
For the prettiest young fair maid
    That ever was seen;
We'll wash her in new milk
    And clothe her in silk,
And write down her name
    With a gold pen and ink.

Bagpipes

Puss came dancing out of a barn
With a pair of bagpipes under her arm;
She could sing nothing but "Fiddle-de-dee,
The mouse has married the bumblebee."
Pipe, cat; dance, mouse;
We'll have a wedding at our good house.

Pit, Pat

Pit, pat, well-a-day,
Little Robin flew away;
Where can little Robin be?
Gone into the cherry tree.

Three Young Rats

Three young rats with black felt hats,
Three young ducks with new straw flats,
Three young dogs with curling tails,
Three young cats with demi-veils,
Went out to walk with two young pigs
In satin vests and sorrel wigs;
But suddenly it chanced to rain,
And so they all went home again.

A Sunshiny Shower

A sunshiny shower
Won't last half an hour.

When It Rains

The more rain, the more rest,
Fine weather's not always best.

Little Sally Waters

Little Sally Waters, sitting in the sun,
Crying and weeping for a young man.
Rise, Sally, rise, wipe off your eyes;
Fly to the east, fly to the west,
Fly to the one that you love best.

Doctor Foster

Doctor Foster went to Gloucester
In a shower of rain;
He stepped in a puddle right up to his middle
And never went there again.

One Misty, Moisty Morning

One misty, moisty morning,
    When cloudy was the weather,
I met a little old man
    Clothed all in leather.

He began to compliment,
    And I began to grin,
How do you do, and how do you do,
    And how do you do again?

Two Pigeons

I had two pigeons bright and gay,
They flew from me the other day.
What was the reason they did go?
I cannot tell, for I do not know.

The Mischievous Raven

A farmer went trotting upon his gray mare,
   Bumpety, bumpety, bump!
With his daughter behind him so rosy and fair,
   Lumpety, lumpety, lump!

A raven cried "Croak!" and they all tumbled down,
   Bumpety, bumpety, bump!
The mare broke her knees and the farmer his crown,
   Lumpety, lumpety, lump!

The mischievous raven flew laughing away,
   Bumpety, bumpety, bump!
And vowed he would serve them the same the
 next day,
   Lumpety, lumpety, lump!

Blow, Wind, Blow

Blow, wind, blow! and go, mill, go!
That the miller may grind his corn;
That the baker may take it,
And into rolls make it,
And bring us some hot in the morn.

Dibbity, Dibbity

Dibbity, dibbity, dibbity, doe,
Give me a pancake
And I'll go.

Dibbity, dibbity, dibbity, ditter,
Please to give me
A bit of fritter.

The Black Hen

Hickety, pickety, my black hen,
She lays eggs for gentlemen;
Gentlemen come every day
To see what my black hen doth lay.

This is the Way

This is the way the ladies ride:
    Tri-tre-tre-tree, tri-tre-tre-tree!
This is the way the ladies ride:
    Tri-tre, tri-tre, tri-tri-tree!

This is the way the gentlemen ride:
    Gallop-a-trot, gallop-a-trot!
This is the way the gentlemen ride:
    Gallop-a-gallop-a-trot!

This is the way the farmers ride:
    Hobbledy-hoy, hobbledy-hoy!
This is the way the farmers ride:
    Hobbledy-hobbledy-hoy!

Sing a Song of Sixpence

Sing a song of sixpence,
    A pocket full of rye;
Four-and-twenty blackbirds
    Baked in a pie.

When the pie was opened,
    The birds began to sing;
Wasn't that a dainty dish
    To set before the king?

The king was in his countinghouse,
    Counting out his money;
The queen was in the parlor,
    Eating bread and honey.

The maid was in the garden,
    Hanging out the clothes,
When down came a blackbird
    And snapped off her nose.

Purple Plums

Purple plums that hang so high,
I shall eat you by and by.

Diddlety, Diddlety, Dumpty

Diddlety, diddlety, dumpty,
The cat ran up a plum tree;
Half a crown
To fetch her down,
Diddlety, diddlety, dumpty.

Queen Caroline

Queen, Queen Caroline,
Washed her hair in turpentine,
Turpentine made it shine,
Queen, Queen Caroline.

This Little Man Lived All Alone

This little man lived all alone,
And he was a man of sorrow;
For, if the weather was fair today,
He was sure it would rain tomorrow.

Shall We Go A-Shearing?

"Old woman, old woman, shall we go a-shearing?"
"Speak a little louder, sir, I'm very hard of hearing."
"Old woman, old woman, shall I kiss you dearly?"
"Thank you very kindly, sir, I hear you very clearly."

Three Ghostesses

Three little ghostesses,
Sitting on postesses,
Eating buttered toastesses,
Greasing their fistesses,
Up to their wristesses,
Oh, what beastesses
To make such feastesses!

Bye, Baby Bunting

Bye, baby bunting,
Daddy's gone a-hunting,
Gone to get a rabbit skin
To wrap the baby bunting in.

The Man in Our Town

There was a man in our town
And he was wondrous wise,
He jumped into a bramble bush
And scratched out both his eyes;
But when he saw his eyes were out,
With all his might and main,
He jumped into another bush
And scratched them in again.

It's Raining

It's raining, it's pouring,
The old man is snoring.
He went to bed with a cold in his head
And he didn't wake up until morning.

Cross-Patch

Cross-patch,
Draw the latch,
Sit by the fire and spin;
Take a cup
And drink it up,
Then call your neighbors in.

Birds of a Feather

Birds of a feather flock together,
And so will pigs and swine;
Rats and mice will have their choice,
And so will I have mine.

Higglety, Pigglety

Higglety, pigglety, pop!
The dog has eaten the mop;
The pig's in a hurry,
The cat's in a flurry,
Higglety, pigglety, pop!

Fears and Tears

Tommy's tears and Mary's fears
Will make them old before their years.

I Saw a Ship a-Sailing

I saw a ship a-sailing,
    A-sailing on the sea;
And, oh, it was all laden
    With pretty things for thee!

There were comfits in the cabin,
    And apples in the hold;
The sails were made of silk,
    And the masts were all of gold.

The four-and-twenty sailors
    That stood upon the decks
Were four-and-twenty white mice
    With chains about their necks.

The captain was a duck
    With a packet on his back;
And when the ship began to move,
    The captain cried, "Quack, quack!"

Tee-Wee's Boat

Little Tee-Wee,
He went to sea,
In an open boat;
And when it was afloat,
The little boat bended,
My story's ended.

Moses

Moses supposes his toeses are roses,
But Moses supposes erroneously;
For nobody's toeses are posies of roses,
As Moses supposes his toeses to be.

Dickory, Dickory, Dare

Dickory, dickory, dare,
The pig flew up in the air;
The man in brown
Soon brought him down,
Dickory, dickory, dare.

The Rugged Rock

Round and round the rugged rock
The ragged rascal ran.
How many R's are there in that?
Now tell me if you can.

Fiddle-de-dee

Fiddle-de-dee, fiddle-de-dee,
The fly has married the humble-bee.
They went to church, and married was she.
The fly has married the humble-bee.

Little Miss

Little miss, pretty miss,
Blessings light upon you!
If I had half a crown a day,
I'd spend it all upon you.

Sulky Sue

Here's Sulky Sue,
What shall we do?
Turn her face to the wall
Till she comes to.

The Little Boy

There was a little boy went into a barn
And lay down on some hay;
An owl came out and flew about,
And the little boy ran away.

Jenny

Hie to the market, Jenny come trot,
Spilled all her buttermilk, every drop,
Every drop and every dram,
Jenny came home with an empty can.

The First of May

The fair maid who, the first of May,
Goes to the fields at break of day,
And washes in dew from the hawthorn tree,
Will ever after handsome be.

At Belle Isle

At the siege of Belle Isle,
I was there all the while,
All the while, all the while,
At the siege of Belle Isle.

To Babylon

How many miles to Babylon?
Three score miles and ten.
Can I get there by candlelight?
Yes, and back again.
If your heels are nimble and light,
You may get there by candlelight.

Cakes and Custard

When Jacky's a good boy,
    He shall have cakes and custard;
But when he does nothing but cry,
    He shall have nothing but mustard.

Green Cheese

Green cheese, yellow laces,
Up and down the market places,
Turn, cheeses, turn!

Jerry Hall

Jerry Hall,
He is so small,
A rat could eat him,
Hat and all.

The Mulberry Bush

Here we go round the mulberry bush,
The mulberry bush, the mulberry bush,
Here we go round the mulberry bush,
On a cold and frosty morning.

This is the way we wash our hands,
Wash our hands, wash our hands,
This is the way we wash our hands,
On a cold and frosty morning.

This is the way we wash our clothes,
Wash our clothes, wash our clothes,
This is the way we wash our clothes,
On a cold and frosty morning.

This is the way we go to school,
Go to school, go to school,
This is the way we go to school,
On a cold and frosty morning.

This is the way we come out of school,
Come out of school, come out of school,
This is the way we come out of school,
On a cold and frosty morning.

John Watts

Pretty John Watts,
We are troubled with rats,
Will you drive them out of the house?
We have mice, too, in plenty,
That feast in the pantry;
But let them stay,
And nibble away:
What harm is a little brown mouse?

One, Two, Buckle My Shoe

One, two, buckle my shoe;
Three, four, shut the door;
Five, six, pick up sticks;
Seven, eight, lay them straight;
Nine, ten, a good fat hen;
Eleven, twelve, dig and delve;
Thirteen, fourteen, maids are courting;
Fifteen, sixteen, maids in the kitchen;
Seventeen, eighteen, maids are waiting;
Nineteen, twenty, my plate's empty.

Hot Boiled Beans

Hot boiled beans and very good butter,
Ladies and gentlemen, come to supper.

Caution

"Mother, may I go out to swim?"
"Yes, my darling daughter.
Hang your clothes on a hickory limb,
But don't go near the water!"

What Can the Matter Be?

Oh, dear, what can the matter be?
Dear, dear, what can the matter be?
Oh, dear, what can the matter be?
Johnny's so long at the fair.

He promised he'd buy me a fairing should please me,
And then for a kiss, oh! he vowed he would tease me,
He promised he'd bring me a bunch of blue ribbons
To tie up my bonny brown hair.

He promised he'd bring me a basket of posies,
A garland of lilies, a garland of roses,
A little straw hat, to set off the blue ribbons
That tie up my bonny brown hair.

Wines and Cakes

Wine and cakes for gentlemen,
Hay and corn for horses,
A cup of ale for good old wives,
And kisses for young lasses.

Doctor Fell

I do not like thee, Doctor Fell;
The reason why, I cannot tell;
But this I know, and know full well,
I do not like thee, Doctor Fell.

The King of France

The King of France went up the hill
With forty thousand men;
The king of France came down the hill,
And ne'er went up again.

A Dog and a Cat

A dog and a cat went out together
To see some friends just out of town.
Said the cat to the dog,
"What d'ye think of the weather?"
"I think, ma'am, the rain will come down,
But don't be alarmed, for I have an umbrella
That will shelter us both," said this amiable fellow.

Bryan O'Lin

Bryan O'Lin had no breeches to wear,
    So he bought him a sheepskin and made him a pair,
With the skinny side out and the woolly side in,
    "A-ha, that is warm!" said Bryan O'Lin.

The Church and the Steeple

Here is the church, and here is the steeple;
Open the door and here are the people.
Here is the parson going upstairs,
And here he is a-saying his prayers.

65

The Old Woman in a Shoe

There was an old woman
    Who lived in a shoe.
She had so many children,
    She didn't know what to do.

She gave them some broth,
    Without any bread,
And spanked them all soundly
    And sent them to bed.

The Man Who Had Naught

There was a man and he had naught,
    And robbers came to rob him;
He crept up to the chimney pot,
    And then they thought they had him.

But he got down on t'other side,
    And then they could not find him;
He ran fourteen miles in fifteen days,
    And never looked behind him.

There Was a Little Girl

There was a little girl, and she had a little curl
    Right in the middle of her forehead.
When she was good, she was very, very good,
    And when she was bad, she was horrid.

Diddle, Diddle Dumpling

Diddle, diddle, dumpling, my son John.
Went to bed with his trousers on;
One shoe off and one shoe on,
Diddle, diddle, dumpling, my son John.

Multiplication is Vexation

Multiplication is vexation,
Division is as bad;
The rule of three perplexes me
And practice drives me mad.

Mother Shuttle

Old Mother Shuttle
Lived in a coal-scuttle
Along with her dog and her cat;
What they ate I can't tell,
But 'tis known very well
That not one of the party was fat.

Old Mother Shuttle
Scoured out her coal-scuttle,
And washed both her dog and her cat;
The cat scratched her nose
So they came to hard blows,
And who was the gainer by that?

The Milkmaid

Little maid, pretty maid,
    Whither goest thou?
Down in the forest
    To milk my cow.
Shall I go with thee?
    No, not now.
When I send for thee,
    Then come thou.

Poor Dog Bright

Poor Dog Bright
Ran off with all his might,
Because the cat was after him —
Poor Dog Bright!

Poor Cat Fright
Ran off with all her might,
Because the dog was after her —
Poor Cat Fright!

The Robin

The north wind doth blow
And we shall have snow,
And what will poor robin do then,
    Poor thing?

He'll sit in a barn
And keep himself warm,
And hide his head under his wing,
    Poor thing!

Tom, Tom, the Piper's Son

Tom, Tom, the piper's son,
Stole a pig, and away he run.
The pig was eat, and Tom was beat,
And Tom ran crying down the street.

Harvest

The boughs do shake and the bells do ring,
So merrily comes our harvest in,
Our harvest in, our harvest in,
So merrily comes our harvest in.

We've ploughed, we've sowed,
We've reaped, we've mowed,
We've got our harvest in.

Ring-a-Ring o' Roses

Ring-a-ring o' roses,
A pocket full of posies,
   A-tishoo! A-tishoo!
We all fall down.

The cows are in the meadow,
Lying fast asleep,
   A-tishoo! A-tishoo!
We all get up again.

Hoddley, Poddley

Hoddley, poddley, puddle and fogs,
Cats are to marry the poodle dogs;
Cats in the blue jackets and dogs in red hats,
What will become of the mice and the rats?

Hush, Little Baby

Hush, little baby, don't say a word,
Papa's going to buy you a mocking bird.

If the mocking bird won't sing,
Papa's going to buy you a diamond ring.

If the diamond ring turns to brass,
Papa's going to buy you a looking-glass.

If the looking-glass gets broke,
Papa's going to buy you a billy-goat.

If that billy-goat runs away,
Papa's going to buy you another today.

Elizabeth

Elizabeth, Libby, Betsy and Bess,
They all went together to seek a bird's nest;
They found a bird's nest with five eggs in,
They all took one, and left four in.

The Man in the Wilderness

The man in the wilderness said to me,
"How many strawberries grow in the sea?"
I answered him as I thought good,
"As many as red herrings grow in the wood."

Days in the Month

Thirty days hath September,
April, June and November;
All the rest have thirty-one,
Excepting February alone,
And that has twenty-eight days clear
And twenty-nine in each leap year.

Poll Parrot

Little Poll Parrot
Sat in his garret,
Eating toast and tea;
A little brown mouse
Jumped into the house
And stole it all away.

Two Little Dogs

Two little dogs sat by the fire
Over a fender of coal-dust;
Said one little dog to the other little dog,
"If you don't talk, why, I must."

Saturday Night

On Saturday night I lost my wife,
And where do you think I found her?
Up in the moon, singing a tune,
And all the stars around her.

See-saw, Sacradown

See-saw, sacradown,
Which is the way to London town?
One foot up and the other foot down,
That is the way to London town.

Wibbleton and Wobbleton

From Wibbleton to Wobbleton is fifteen miles,
From Wobbleton to Wibbleton is fifteen miles,
From Wibbleton to Wobbleton,
From Wobbleton to Wibbleton,
From Wibbleton to Wobbleton is fifteen miles.

Candle Saving

To make your candles last for aye,
You wives and maids give ear-o!
To put them out is the only way,
Says Honest John Boldero.

Going to St. Ives

As I was going to St. Ives,
I met a man with seven wives;
Each wife had seven sacks,
Each sack had seven cats,
Each cat had seven kits.
Kits, cats, sacks and wives,
How many were going to St. Ives?

The Moon

I see the moon,
And the moon sees me;
God bless the moon,
And God bless
Me.

The Star

Twinkle, twinkle, little star,
How I wonder what you are!
Up above the world so high,
Like a diamond in the sky.

Girls and Boys, Come Out to Play

Girls and boys,
    Come out to play,
The moon doth shine
    As bright as day.
Leave your supper
    And leave your sleep,
And come with your playfellows
    Into the street.
Come with a whoop,
    Come with a call,
Come with a good will
    Or not at all.
Up the ladder
    And down the wall,
A halfpenny roll
    will serve us all;
You find milk
    And I'll find flour,
And we'll have a pudding
    In half an hour.

Ten Little Bluebirds

Ten little bluebirds, perched on a pine;
One flew away and then there were nine.

Nine little bluebirds, sitting up late;
One flew away and then there were eight.

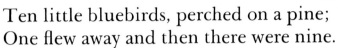
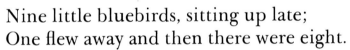

Eight little bluebirds, looking high to heaven;
One flew away and then there were seven.

Seven little bluebirds, picking up sticks;
One flew away and then there were six.

Six little bluebirds, glad to be alive;
One flew away and then there were five.

Five little bluebirds, sitting on a door;
One flew away and then there were four.

Four little bluebirds, singing merrily;
One flew away and then there were three.

Three little bluebirds, hidden in a shoe;
One flew away and then there were two.

Two little bluebirds, pecking at a crumb;
One flew away and then there was one.

One little bluebird, chirping in the sun;
He flew away and then there were none.

77

The House That Jack Built

This is the house that Jack built.

This is the malt
That lay in the house that Jack built.

This is the rat,
That ate the malt
That lay in the house that Jack built.

This is the cat,
That killed the rat,
That ate the malt
That lay in the house that Jack built.

This is the dog,
That worried the cat,
That killed the rat,
That ate the malt
That lay in the house that Jack built.

This is the cow with the crumpled horn,
That tossed the dog,
That worried the cat,
That killed the rat,
That ate the malt
That lay in the house that Jack built.

This is the maiden all forlorn,
That milked the cow with the crumpled horn,
That tossed the dog,
That worried the cat,
That killed the rat,
That ate the malt
That lay in the house that Jack built.

This is the man all tattered and torn,
That kissed the maiden all forlorn,
That milked the cow with the crumpled horn,
That tossed the dog,
That worried the cat,
That killed the rat,
That ate the malt
That lay in the house that Jack built.

This is the priest all shaven and shorn,
That married the man all tattered and torn,
That kissed the maiden all forlorn,
That milked the cow with the crumpled horn,
That tossed the dog,
That worried the cat,
That killed the rat,
That ate the malt
That lay in the house that Jack built.

This is the cock that crowed in the morn,
That waked the priest all shaven and shorn,
That married the man all tattered and torn,
That kissed the maiden all forlorn,
That milked the cow with the crumpled horn,
That tossed the dog,
That worried the cat,
That killed the rat,
That ate the malt
That lay in the house that Jack built.

This is the farmer sowing his corn,
That kept the cock that crowed in the morn,
That waked the priest all shaven and shorn,
That married the man all tattered and torn,
That kissed the maiden all forlorn,
That milked the cow with the crumpled horn,
That tossed the dog,
That worried the cat,
That killed the rat,
That ate the malt
That lay in the house that Jack built.

Race Starting

Bell horses, bell horses,
　　What time of day?
One o'clock, two o'clock,
　　Three and away.

One to make ready,
　　And two to prepare;
Good luck to the rider,
　　And away goes the mare.

One for the money,
　　Two for the show,
Three to make ready,
　　And four and go.

Hot Cross Buns

Hot cross buns, hot cross buns,
One a penny, two a penny,
Hot cross buns.
If you have no daughters,
Give them to your sons;
One a penny, two a penny,
Hot cross buns.

The Greedy Man

The greedy man is he who sits
　　And bites bits out of plates,
Or else takes up an almanac
　　And gobbles all the dates.

That's All

There was an old woman sat spinning,
And that's the first beginning;
She had a calf,
And that's half;
She took it by the tail,
And threw it over the wall,
And that's all.

Pussy Sits Beside the Fire

Pussy sits beside the fire; how can she be so fair?
In walks the little dog; says, "Pussy, are you there?
How do you do, Mistress Pussy, tell me, how do you do?"
"I thank you kindly, little dog; I fare as well as you."

To the Ladybird

Ladybird, ladybird,
    Fly away home,
Your house is on fire
    And your children all gone;
All except one,
    And that's little Ann,
And she has crept under
    The warming pan.

Tommy Trot

Tommy Trot, a man of law,
Sold his bed and lay upon straw;
Sold his straw and slept on grass
To buy his wife a looking-glass.

My Little Dog

Oh where, oh where has my little dog gone?
    Oh where, oh where can he be?
With his ears cut short and his tail cut long,
    Oh, where, oh where is he?

Little Maiden

Little maiden, better tarry;
Time enough next year to marry.
Hearts may change,
And so may fancy;
Wait a little longer, Nancy.

Good Night

Good night,
Sweet repose,
Half the bed
And all the clothes.

Little Bo-Peep

Little Bo-Peep has lost her sheep,
    And can't tell where to find them.
Leave them alone, and they'll come home,
    And bring their tails behind them.

Little Bo-Peep fell fast asleep,
    And dreamed she heard them bleating,
But when she awoke, she found it a joke,
    For they were still a-fleeting.

Then up she took her little crook,
    Determined for to find them;
She found them, indeed, but it made her heart bleed,
    For they'd left all their tails behind them.

It happened one day, as Bo-Peep did stray
    Into a meadow hard by;
There she espied their tails, side by side,
    All hung on a tree to dry.

She heaved a sigh and wiped her eye,
    And over the hillocks she raced;
And tried what she could, as a shepherdess should,
    That each tail be properly placed.

Daffodils

Daffy-down-dilly has come to town
In a yellow petticoat and a green gown.

Niddle-Noddle

Little Robin Redbreast
Sat upon a rail;
Niddle-noddle went his head,
Wiggle-waggle went his tail.

The Queen of Hearts

The Queen of Hearts
She made some tarts,
All on a summer's day;
The Knave of Hearts
He stole some tarts
And took them clean away.

The King of Hearts
Called for the tarts,
And beat the Knave full sore;
The Knave of Hearts
Brought back the tarts,
And vowed he'd steal no more.

Nothing-at-All

There was an old woman called Nothing-at-All,
Who lived in a dwelling exceedingly small;
A man stretched his mouth to its utmost extent,
And down at one gulp house and old woman went.

Davy Dumpling

Davy Davy Dumpling,
Boil him in the pot;
Sugar him and butter him,
And eat him while he's hot.

Pins

See a pin and pick it up,
All the day you'll have good luck.
See a pin and let it lay,
Bad luck you'll have all the day.

The Wind

My lady Wind, my lady Wind,
Went round the house to find
   A chink to set her foot in;
She tried the keyhole in the door,
She tried the crevice in the floor,
   And drove the chimney soot in.

To Market, to Market

To market, to market, to buy a fat pig,
   Home again, home again, jiggety jig.
To market, to market, to buy a fat hog,
   Home again, home again, jiggety jog.
To market, to market, to buy a hot bun,
   Home again, home again, market is done.

Taffy was a Welshman

Taffy was a Welshman, Taffy was a thief;
Taffy came to my house and stole a piece of beef;
I went to Taffy's house, Taffy wasn't home;
Taffy came to my house and stole a marrow-bone.

I went to Taffy's house, Taffy wasn't in;
Taffy came to my house and stole a silver pin;
I went to Taffy's house, Taffy was in bed;
I took up the marrow-bone and flung it at his head.

Little Bird

Once I saw a little bird
 Come hop, hop, hop,
And I cried, "Little bird,
 Will you stop, stop, stop?"

I was going to the window
 To say, "How do you do?"
But he shook his little tail
 And away he flew.

Blind Man's Buff

Blind man, blind man,
 Sure you can't see?
Turn round three times,
 And try to catch me.
Turn east, turn west,
 Catch as you can,
Did you think you'd caught me?
 Blind, blind man!

The Milk Maid

"Where are you going, my pretty maid?"
"I'm going a-milking, sir," she said.

"May I go with you, my pretty maid?"
"You're kindly welcome, sir," she said.

"What is your father, my pretty maid?"
"My father's a farmer, sir," she said.

"What is your fortune, my pretty maid?"
"My face is my fortune, sir," she said.

"Then I can't marry you, my pretty maid."
"Nobody asked you, sir," she said.

Hickory, Dickory, Dock

Hickory, dickory, dock!
The mouse ran up the clock;
The clock struck one,
The mouse ran down,
Hickory, dickory, dock!

Lavender's Blue

Lavender's blue, diddle, diddle,
    Lavender's green;
When I am king, diddle, diddle,
    You shall be queen.

Let the birds sing, diddle, diddle,
    And the lambs play;
We shall be safe, diddle, diddle,
    Out of harm's way.

This Little Pig

This little pig went to market;
This little pig stayed at home;
This little pig had roast beef;
This little pig had none;
This little pig cried "Wee, wee, wee,
I can't find my way home."

This Old Man

This old man, he played one,
He played knick-knack on his thumb,
Knick-knack, paddy whack,
Give the dog a bone,
This old man came rolling home.

This old man, he played two,
He played knick-knack on his shoe,
Knick-knack, paddy whack,
Give the dog a bone,
This old man came rolling home.

This old man, he played three,
He played knick-knack on his knee,
Knick-knack, paddy whack,
Give the dog a bone,
This old man came rolling home.

Gregory Griggs

Gregory Griggs, Gregory Griggs,
Had twenty-seven different wigs.
He wore them up, he wore them down,
To please the people of the town;
He wore them east, he wore them west,
But he never could tell which he loved the best.

Fire! Fire!

"Fire! Fire!" said Mrs. Dyer.
"Where? Where?" said Mrs. Dare.
"Down the town," said Mrs. Brown.
"Any damage?" said Mrs. Gamage.
"None at all," said Mrs. Hall.

Banbury Cross

Ride a cock-horse to Banbury Cross,
To see a fine lady upon a white horse;
Rings on her fingers and bells on her toes,
She shall have music wherever she goes.

The Jolly Miller

There was a jolly miller once,
        Lived on the river Dee;
He worked and sang from morn till night,
        No lark so blithe as he.
And this the burden of his song
        Forever used to be,
"I care for nobody — no! not I,
        Since nobody cares for me."

A Nick and a Nock

A nick and a nock
A hen and a cock
And a penny for my master.

Magic Words

Hearts, like doors, will open with ease
To very, very little keys,
And don't forget that two of these
Are "I thank you" and "If you please."

89

Three Wise Men of Gotham

Three wise men of Gotham
Went to sea in a bowl,
And if the bowl had been stronger,
My song would have been longer.

If

If all the seas were one sea,
What a great sea that would be!
If all the trees were one tree,
What a great tree that would be!
And if all the axes were one axe,
What a great axe that would be!
And if all the men were one man,
What a great man that would be!
And if the great man took the great axe,
And cut down the great tree,
And let it fall into the great sea,
What a splish-splash that would be!

Little King Pippin

Little King Pippin, he built a fine hall,
Pie crust and pastry crust, that was the wall;
The windows were made of black pudding and
    white,
And slated with pancakes, you ne'er saw the like.

See-Saw, Margery Daw

See-saw, Margery Daw,
Jacky shall have a new master;
He shall have but a penny a day,
Because he can't work any faster.

Man of Derby

A little old man of Derby,
How do you think he served me?
He took away my bread and cheese,
And that is how he served me.

Pairs or Pears

Twelve pairs hanging high,
Twelve knights riding by;
Each knight took a pear
And yet left a dozen there.

The Key of the Kingdom

This is the key of the kingdom:
In that kingdom is a city,
In that city is a town,
In that town there is a street,
In that street there winds a lane,
In that lane there is a yard,
In that yard there is a house,
In that house there waits a room,
In that room there is a bed,
On that bed there is a basket,
    A basket of flowers.

Flowers in the basket,
Basket on the bed,
Bed in the chamber,
Chamber in the house,
House in the weedy yard,
Yard in the winding lane,
Lane in the broad street,
Street in the high town,
Town in the city,
City in the kingdom:
    This is the key of the kingdom.

Terence McDiddler

Terence McDiddler,
    The three-stringed fiddler,
Can charm, if you please,
    The fish from the seas.

I Had a Little Moppet

I had a little moppet,
I kept it in my pocket
And fed it on corn and hay;
Then came a proud beggar
And said he would wed her,
And stole my little moppet away.

Old Chairs to Mend

If I'd as much money as I could spend,
I never would cry, "Old chairs to mend,
Old chairs to mend, old chairs to mend."
I never would cry, "Old chairs to mend."

If I'd as much money as I could tell,
I never would cry, "Old clothes to sell,
Old clothes to sell, old clothes to sell."
I never would cry, "Old clothes to sell."

Hector Protector

Hector Protector was dressed all in green;
Hector Protector was sent to the Queen.
The Queen did not like him,
No more did the King;
So Hector Protector was sent back again.

I Sing, I Sing

I sing, I sing,
From morn till night;
From cares I'm free
And my heart is light.

Yankee Doodle

Yankee Doodle came to town,
    Riding on a pony;
He stuck a feather in his cap
    And called it macaroni.

Little Fishes

Little fishes in a brook,
Father caught them on a hook,
Mother fried them in a pan,
Johnny eats them like a man.

Little Betty Blue

Little Betty Blue
Lost her holiday shoe;
What can little Betty do?
Give her another
To match the other,
And then she may walk out in two.

Six Little Mice

Six little mice sat down to spin;
Pussy passed by and she peeped in.
"What are you doing, my little men?"
"Weaving coats for gentlemen."
"Shall I come in and cut off your threads?"
"No, no, Mistress Pussy, you'd bite off our heads."
"Oh, no, I'll not; I'll help you to spin."
"That may be so, but you don't come in!"

Dame Trot

Dame Trot and her cat
   Sat down for a chat,
The Dame sat on this side
   And Puss sat on that.

"Puss," says the Dame,
   "Can you catch a rat,
Or a mouse in the dark?"
   "Purr," says the cat.

Dame Trot and her cat
   Led a peaceable life
When they were not troubled
   With other folks' strife.

When Dame had her dinner,
   Pussy would wait,
And was sure to receive
   A nice piece from her plate.

Poor Old Robinson Crusoe

Poor old Robinson Crusoe!
Poor old Robinson Crusoe!
   They made him a coat
   Of an old nanny goat,
I wonder how they could do so!
   With a ring-a-ting-tang
   And a ring-a-ting-tang,
Poor old Robinson Crusoe!

The Ten O'clock Scholar

A dillar, a dollar, a ten o'clock scholar!
   What makes you come so soon?
You used to come at ten o'clock,
   But now you come at noon.

I Had a Little Nut Tree

I had a little nut tree,
  Nothing would it bear
But a silver nutmeg
  And a golden pear.
The King of Spain's daughter
  Came to visit me,
And all for the sake
  Of my little nut tree.
I skipped over water,
  I danced over sea,
And all the birds in the air
  Couldn't catch me.

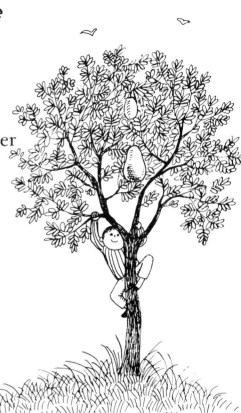

Burnie Bee

Burnie bee, burnie bee,
Tell me when your wedding be?
If it be tomorrow day,
Take your wings and fly away.

Hark! Hark!

Hark! Hark! The dogs do bark.
  Beggars are coming to town:
Some in jags and some in rags,
  And one in a velvet gown.

Lazy Mary

"Lazy Mary, will you get up,
Will you get up, will you get up,
Lazy Mary, will you get up,
Will you get up today?"

"No, Mother, I won't get up,
I won't get up, I won't get up,
No, Mother, I won't get up,
I won't get up today!"

97

Robin Redbreast

Little Robin Redbreast
    Sat upon a tree,
Up went pussy cat,
    And down went he;
Down came pussy,
    And away Robin ran;
Says little Robin Redbreast,
    "Catch me if you can."

Little Robin Redbreast
    Jumped upon a wall,
Pussy cat jumped after him,
    And almost got a fall;
Little Robin chirped and sang,
    And what did pussy say?
Pussy cat said, "Mew!"
    And Robin jumped away.

Little Miss Muffet

Little Miss Muffet sat on a tuffet,
Eating her curds and whey;
Along came a spider
    who sat down beside her
And frightened Miss Muffet away.

Mary, Mary, Quite Contrary

Mary, Mary, quite contrary,
    How does your garden grow?
With silver bells and cockle shells
    And pretty maids all in a row.

Come Hither

"Come hither, little puppy dog;
    I'll give you a new collar,
If you will learn to read your book
    And be a clever scholar."

"No, no!" replied the puppy dog,
    "I've other fish to fry,
For I must learn to guard your house
    And bark when thieves come nigh!"

"Come hither, pretty cockatoo;
    Come and learn your letters,
And you shall have a knife and fork
    To eat with, like your betters."

"No, no!" the cockatoo replied,
    "My beak will do as well;
I'd rather eat my victuals thus
    Than go and learn to spell."

"Come hither, little pussy cat;
    If you'll your grammar study,
I'll give you silver clogs to wear
    Whene'er the gutter's muddy."

"No! whilst I grammar learn," says Puss,
    "Your house will, in a trice,
Be overrun from top to bottom
    With flocks of rats and mice."

Lucy Locket

Lucy Locket lost her pocket,
Kitty Fisher found it;
Not a penny was there in it,
Only ribbon round it.

100

There Was an Owl

There was an owl lived in an oak,
 Wisky, wasky, weedle;
And all the words he ever spoke
 Were fiddle, faddle, feedle.

A sportsman chanced to come that way,
 Wisky, wasky, weedle;
Says he, "I'll shoot you, silly bird,
 So fiddle, faddle, feedle!"

The Donkey

Donkey, donkey, old and gray,
Ope your mouth and gently bray;
Lift your ears and blow your horn,
To wake the world this sleepy morn.

John Fought for His Beloved Land

John fought for his beloved land,
And when the war was over,
He kept a little cookie stand
And lived and died in clover.

Anna Maria

Anna Maria, she sat on the fire;
The fire was too hot, she sat on the pot;
The pot was too round, she sat on the ground;
The ground was too flat, she sat on the cat;
The cat ran away with Maria on her back.

Wash the Dishes

Wash the dishes, wipe the dishes,
Ring the bell for tea;
Three good wishes, three good kisses,
I will give to thee.

Old Mother Hubbard

Old Mother Hubbard went to the cupboard
To get her poor dog a bone;
But when she got there, the cupboard was bare,
And so the poor dog had none.

She went to the barber's to buy him a wig;
When she came back, he was dancing a jig.
"Oh, you dear merry Grig! How nicely you're prancing!'
Then she held up the wig, and he began dancing.

She went to the fruiterer's to buy him some fruit;
When she came back, he was playing the flute.
"Oh, you musical dog! You surely can speak!
Come, sing me a song!" . . . and he set up a squeak.

The dog, he cut capers and turned out his toes;
'Twill soon cure the vapors, such attitude shows.
The dame made a curtsy, the dog made a bow;
The dame said, "Your servant!" The dog said, "Bow-wow!"

Mary Had a Little Lamb

Mary had a little lamb,
 Its fleece was white as snow;
And everywhere that Mary went,
 The lamb was sure to go.

It followed her to school one day,
 That was against the rule;
It made the children laugh and play
 To see a lamb at school.

And so the teacher turned it out,
 But still it lingered near;
And waited patiently about
 Till Mary did appear.

"Why does the lamb love Mary so?"
 The eager children cry.
"Why, Mary loves the lamb, you know,"
 The teacher did reply.

The Pumpkin Eater

Peter, Peter, pumpkin eater,
Had a wife and couldn't keep her;
He put her in a pumpkin shell
And there he kept her very well.

Peter, Peter, pumpkin eater,
Had another, and didn't love her;
Peter learned to read and spell,
And then he loved her very well.

The Muffin Man

Oh, do you know the muffin man?
Oh, do you know his name?
Oh, do you know the muffin man
Who lives in Drury Lane?

Oh, yes, I know the muffin man,
The muffin man, the muffin man,
Oh, yes, I know the muffin man
Who lives in Drury Lane.

Peter White's Nose

Peter White will ne'er go right;
Would you know the reason why?
He follows his nose wherever he goes,
And that stands all awry.

Georgie Porgie

Georgie Porgie, pudding and pie,
Kissed the girls and made them cry;
When the boys came out to play,
Georgie Porgie ran away.

Betty Botter's Batter

Betty Botter bought some butter,
"But," she said, "the butter's bitter;
If I put it in my batter,
It will make my batter bitter,
But a bit of better butter,
That would make my batter better."
So she bought a bit of butter,
Better than her bitter butter,
And she put it in her batter,
And the batter was not bitter.
So t'was better Betty Botter
Bought a bit of better butter.

Hob, Shoe, Hob

Hob, shoe, hob,
Hob, shoe, hob,
Here's a nail and there's a nail,
And that's well shod.

A Week of Birthdays

Monday's child is fair of face,
Tuesday's child is full of grace,
Wednesday's child is full of woe,
Thursday's child has far to go,
Friday's child is loving and giving,
Saturday's child works hard for a living,
And the child that's born on the Sabbath day
Is bonny and blithe, and good and gay.

Goose Feathers

Cackle, cackle, Mother Goose,
Have you any feathers loose?
Truly have I, pretty fellow,
Half enough to fill a pillow.
Here are quills, take one or two,
And down to make a bed for you.

Run, Boys, Run

Rats in the garden, catch 'em, Towser,
Cows in the cornfield, run, boys, run;
Cat's in the cream pot, stop her, now, sir,
Fire on the mountain, run, boys, run.

Hobbledy Hops

Hobbledy Hops,
He made some tops
    Out of the morning glory;
He used the seed —
He did, indeed,
    And that's the end of my story.

As I Was Going Along

As I was going along, long, long,
A-singing a comical song, song, song,
The lane that I went was so long, long, long,
And the song that I sung was as long, long, long,
And so I went singing along.

Old Woman, Old Woman

There was an old woman tossed up in a blanket,
    Nineteen times as high the moon;
Where she was going I couldn't but ask it,
    For under her arm she carried a broom.

"Old woman, old woman, old woman," said I,
    "Whither, oh whither, oh whither so high?"
"To sweep the cobwebs from the sky,
    And I'll be with you by and by."

Wee Willie Winkie

Wee Willie Winkie runs through the town,
Upstairs and downstairs, in his nightgown,
Rapping at the window, crying through the lock,
"Are the children in their beds? Now it's eight o'clock."

Star Light

Star light, star bright,
First star I see tonight,
I wish I may, I wish I might,
Have the wish I wish tonight.

Bedtime

The Man in the Moon looked out of the moon,
And this is what he said:
" 'Tis time that, now I'm getting up,
All children are in bed."

A Candle

Little Nanny Etticoat
In a white petticoat
And a red nose;
The longer she stands,
The shorter she grows.

The Mist

A hill full, a hole full,
Yet you cannot catch a bowl full.

Kindness

I love little pussy,
    Her coat is so warm,
And if I don't hurt her,
    She'll do me no harm.

So I'll not pull her tail,
    Nor drive her away,
But pussy and I
    Very gently will play.

She shall sit by my side
    And I'll give her some food;
And pussy will love me
    Because I am good.

Handy Dandy

Handy dandy, riddledy ro,
Which hand will you have, high or low?

Come Tie My Cravat

Jeanie come tie my,
Jeanie come tie my,
Jeanie come tie my bonnie cravat;
I've tied it behind,
I've tied it before,
And I've tied it so often, I'll tie it no more.

A Chimney

Black within and red without,
Four corners round about.

Shoe a Little Horse

Shoe a little horse,
Shoe a little mare,
But let the little colt
Go bare, bare, bare.

I Love Sixpence

I love sixpence, pretty little sixpence,
I love sixpence better than my life;
I spent a penny of it, I spent another,
And I took fourpence home to my wife.

Oh, my little fourpence, pretty little fourpence,
I love fourpence better than my life;
I spent a penny of it, I spent another,
And I took twopence home to my wife.

Oh, my little twopence, pretty little twopence,
I love twopence better than my life;
I spent a penny of it, I spent another,
And I took nothing home to my wife.

Oh, my little nothing, my pretty little nothing,
What will nothing buy for my wife?
I have nothing, I spent nothing,
I love nothing better than my wife.

The Bad Rider

I had a little pony,
     His name was Dapple Gray;
I lent him to a lady
     To ride a mile away.
She whipped him, she slashed him,
     She rode him through the mire;
I would not lend my pony now
     For all the lady's hire.

If All the World

If all the world were apple pie,
     And all the sea were ink,
And all the trees were bread and cheese,
     What would we have to drink?

Great A, Little a

Great A, little a,
Bouncing B!
The cat's in the cupboard
And can't see me.

Three Little Kittens

Three little kittens
They lost their mittens,
    And they began to cry,
"Oh, Mother dear,
We sadly fear
    That we have lost our mittens."
"What, lost your mittens!
You naughty kittens!
    Then you shall have no pie."
Mee-ow, mee-ow, mee-ow.
No, you shall have no pie.

The three little kittens
They found their mittens,
    And they began to cry,
"Oh, Mother dear,
See here, see here,
    For we have found our mittens."
"Put on your mittens,
You silly kittens,
    And you shall have some pie."
    Purr-r, purr-r, purr-r,
    Oh, let us have some pie.

The three little kittens
Put on their mittens
    And soon ate up the pie;
"Oh, Mother dear,
We greatly fear
    That we have soiled our mittens."
"What, soiled your mittens!
You naughty kittens!"
    Then they began to sigh.
    Mee-ow, mee-ow, mee-ow.
    Then they began to sigh.

The three little kittens
They washed their mittens,
    And hung them out to dry;
"Oh, Mother dear,
Do you not hear
    That we have washed our mittens?"
"What, washed your mittens!
Then you're good kittens,
    But I smell a rat close by."
    Mee-ow, mee-ow, mee-ow.
    We smell a rat close by.

Curly-Locks

Curly-Locks, Curly-Locks,
    Wilt thou be mine?
Thou shall not wash dishes
    Nor yet feed the swine;
But sit on a cushion
    And sew a fine seam,
And feed upon strawberries,
    Sugar and cream.

Humpty-Dumpty

Humpty Dumpty sat on a wall,
Humpty Dumpty had a great fall;
All the King's horses and all the King's men
Couldn't put Humpty together again.

Jumping Joan

Here am I,
Little Jumping Joan;
When nobody's with me,
I'm all alone.

Two Little Blackbirds

As I went over the water,
    The water went over me.
I saw two little blackbirds
    Sitting on a tree;
One called me a rascal,
    And one called me a thief,
I took up my little black stick
    And knocked out all their teeth.

Friday Night's Dream

Friday night's dream
On the Saturday told
Is sure to come true,
Be it ever so old.

111

The Spider and the Fly

"Will you walk into my parlor?"
　　Said the spider to the fly;
" 'Tis the prettiest little parlor
　　That ever you did spy.
The way into my parlor
　　Is up a winding stair,
And I have many curious things
　　To show when you are there."
"Oh, no, no," said the little fly.
　　"To ask me is in vain,
For who goes up your winding stair
　　Can ne'er come down again!"

Sneeze On Monday

Sneeze on Monday, sneeze for danger;
Sneeze on Tuesday, kiss a stranger;
Sneeze on Wednesday, get a letter;
Sneeze on Thursday, something better;
Sneeze on Friday, sneeze for sorrow;
Sneeze on Saturday, joy tomorrow.

I Had a Little Husband

I had a little husband,
　　No bigger than my thumb;
I put him in a pint-pot
　　And there I bade him drum.

I bought a little horse
　　That galloped up and down;
I bridled him, and saddled him,
　　And sent him out of town.

I gave him some garters
　　To garter up his hose,
And a little silk handkerchief
　　To wipe his pretty nose.

The Clock

There's a neat little clock,
In the schoolroom it stands,
And it points to the time
With its two little hands.

And may we, like the clock,
Keep a face clean and bright,
With hands every ready
To do what is right.

If Wishes Were Horses

If wishes were horses,
Beggars would ride;
If turnips were watches,
I'd wear one by my side;
And if IF'S and AND'S
Were pots and pans,
There'd be no work for tinkers!

Jack, Be Nimble

Jack, be nimble; Jack, be quick;
Jack, jump over the candlestick.

The Teeth

Thirty white horses
Upon a red hill;
Now they stamp,
Now they champ,
Now they stand still.

Little Boy Blue

Little Boy Blue,
  Come blow your horn!
The sheep's in the meadow,
  The cow's in the corn.
Where is the boy
  Who looks after the sheep?
He's under a haystack,
  Fast asleep.
Will you wake him?
  No, not I,
For if I do,
  He'll be sure to cry.

Bob Robin

Little Bob Robin,
Where do you live?
Up in yonder wood, sir,
On a hazel twig.

Tommy Tittlemouse

Little Tommy Tittlemouse
Lived in a little house;
He caught fishes
In other men's ditches.

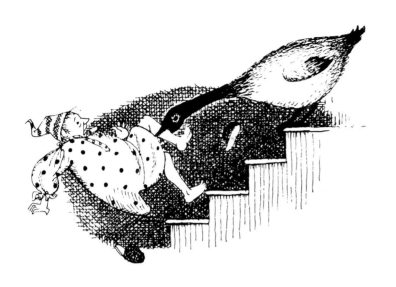

Goosey, Goosey, Gander

Goosey, goosey, gander,
    Whither shall I wander?
Upstairs and downstairs
    And in my lady's chamber.

There I met an old man
    Who would not say his prayers;
I took him by the left leg
    And threw him down the stairs.

Hey, My Kitten

Hey, my kitten, my kitten,
    And hey, my kitten, my deary!
Such a sweet pet as this
    Was neither far nor neary.

Here we go up, up, up,
    Here we go down, down, downy;
Here we go backwards and forwards,
    And here we go round, round, roundy.

Polly Flinders

Little Polly Flinders
Sat among the cinders,
Warming her pretty little toes;
Her mother came and caught her,
And spanked her little daughter
For spoiling her nice new clothes.

Leg Over Leg

Leg over leg,
As the dog went to Dover;
When he came to a stile,
Jump, he went over.

Billy Boy

Oh where have you been, Billy Boy, Billy Boy,
Oh where have you been, charming Billy?
I have been to seek a wife,
She's the joy of my life,
She's a young thing and cannot leave her mother.

Can she bake a cherry pie, Billy Boy, Billy Boy,
Can she bake a cherry pie, charming Billy?
She can bake a cherry pie
Quick as the cat can wink its eye,
She's a young thing and cannot leave her mother.

How old is she, Billy Boy, Billy Boy,
How old is she, charming Billy?
Four times six and eight times seven,
Forty-nine plus eleven,
She's a young thing and cannot leave her mother.

My Maid Mary

My maid Mary,
She minds the dairy,
While I go a-hoeing and mowing each morn;
Merrily run the reel,
And the little spinning wheel,
Whilst I am singing and mowing my corn.

Handy Pandy

Handy Pandy, Jack-a-dandy,
Loves plum cake and sugar candy.
He bought some at a grocer's shop,
And out he came, hop, hop, hop.

There Was a Bee

There was a bee
Sat on a wall,
And "Buzz!" said he,
And that was all.

Rain

Rain on the green grass,
And rain on the tree,
Rain on the house-top,
But not on me.

Lengthening Days

As the days grow longer,
The storms grow stronger.

Little Jack Horner

Little Jack Horner
Sat in the corner,
Eating his Christmas pie;
He put in his thumb
And pulled out a plum,
And said, "What a good boy am I!"

Tommy and Bessy

As Tommy Snooks and Bessy Brooks
    Were walking out one Sunday,
Says Tommy Snooks to Bessy Brooks,
    "Tomorrow will be Monday."

Little Blue Ben

Little Blue Ben, who lives in the glen,
Keeps a blue cat and one blue hen,
Which lays of blue eggs a score and ten;
Where shall I find the little Blue Ben?

Tweedledum and Tweedledee

Tweedledum and Tweedledee
   Agreed to have a battle
For Tweedledum said Tweedledee
   Had spoiled his nice new rattle.

Just then flew by a monstrous crow
   As black as a tar barrel,
Which frightened both the heroes so,
   They quite forgot their quarrel.

The Hobby Horse

I had a little hobby horse,
   And it was dapple gray;
Its head was made of pea-straw,
   Its tail was made of hay.

I sold it to a woman
   For a copper groat;
And I'll not sing my song again
   Without another coat.

All Work and No Play

All work and no play makes Jack a dull boy;
All play and no work makes Jack a mere toy.

Three Blind Mice

Three blind mice, see how they run!
They all ran after the farmer's wife,
Who cut off their tails with a carving knife.
Did you ever see such a sight in your life
As three blind mice?

Pop Goes the Weasel

Up and down the City Road,
    In and out the Eagle,
That's the way the money goes,
    Pop goes the weasel!

Half a pound of tuppenny rice,
    Half a pound of treacle,
Mix it up and make it nice,
    Pop goes the weasel!

Every night when I go out,
    The monkey's on the table;
Take a stick and knock it off,
    Pop goes the weasel!

The Kilkenny Cats

There were once two cats of Kilkenny.
Each thought there was one cat too many;
So they fought and they fit,
And they scratched and they bit,
    Till, excepting their nails,
    And the tips of their tails,
Instead of two cats, there weren't any.

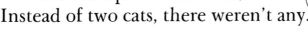

Little Jack Pumpkin Face

Little Jack Pumpkin Face
    Lived on a vine;
Little Jack Pumpkin Face
    Thought it was fine.

First he was small and green,
    Then big and yellow;
Little Jack Pumpkin Face
    Is a fine fellow.

Tea Time

Polly put the kettle on,
Polly put the kettle on,
Polly put the kettle on,
    We'll all have tea.

Sukey take it off again,
Sukey take it off again,
Sukey take it off again,
    They've all gone away.

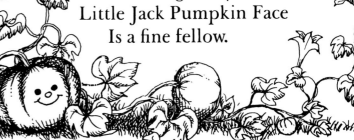

Bow-Wow-Wow!

Bow-wow-wow!
　　Whose dog art thou?
Little Tom Tucker's dog,
　　Bow-wow-wow!

The Owl

A wise old owl sat in an oak,
The more he heard, the less he spoke;
The less he spoke, the more he heard.
Why aren't we all like that wise old bird?

By Myself

As I walked by myself
And talked to myself,
   Myself said unto me,
"Look to thyself,
Take care of thyself,
   For nobody cares for thee."

I answered myself
And said to myself,
   In the selfsame repartee,
"Look to thyself
Or not to thyself,
   The selfsame thing will be."

Ride Away, Ride Away

Ride away, ride away,
    Johnny shall ride,
He shall have a pussycat
    Tied to one side;
He shall have a little dog
    Tied to the other,
And Johnny shall ride
    To see his grandmother.

The Cuckoo

The cuckoo comes in April,
He sings his song in May;
    In the middle of June
    He changes his tune,
And then he flies away.

Little Girl

"Little girl, little girl, where have you been?"
"Gathering roses to give to the Queen."
"Little girl, little girl, what gave she you?"
"She gave me a diamond as big as my shoe."

Hay is for Horses

Hay is for horses,
    Straw is for cows,
Milk is for little pigs,
    And wash for old sows.

For Every Evil

For every evil under the sun,
There is a remedy or there is none.
If there be one, try and find it;
If there be none, never mind it.

Do You Love Me?

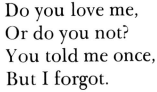

Do you love me,
Or do you not?
You told me once,
But I forgot.

Christmas is Coming

Christmas is coming,
    The geese are getting fat,
Please to put a penny
    In the old man's hat;
If you haven't got a penny,
    A ha'penny will do,
If you haven't got a ha'penny,
    Then God bless you.

Bedtime

"Come, let's to bed,"
Says Sleepy-head;
"Tarry a while," says Slow;
"Put on the pan,"
Says Greedy Nan,
"Let's sup before we go."

And Now, Good Night

And now, good night;
    Our play is done;
Farewell to each
    And every one.

Index of First Lines

Page

A

A, B, C, D, E, F, G	30
A dillar, a dollar, a ten o'clock scholar	96
A dog and a cat went out together	65
A duck and a drake	38
A farmer went trotting upon his gray mare	52
A hill full, a hole full	107
A little old man of Derby	92
A nick and a nock	89
A robin and a robin's son	38
A sunshiny shower	50
A swarm of bees in May	45
A wise old owl sat in an oak	123
All work and no play makes Jack a dull boy	120
And now, good night	125
Anna Maria, she sat on the fire	101
As I walked by myself	99
As I was going along, long, long	105
As I was going to Banbury upon a summer's day	20
As I was going to St. Ives	73
As I went over the water	111
As I went through the garden gap	21
As the days grow longer	118
As Tommy Snooks and Bessy Brooks	119
At Brill on the hill	25
At the siege of Belle Isle	61

B

Baa, baa, black sheep	43
Barber, barber, shave a pig	23
Bat, bat, come under my hat	37
Bell horses, bell horses	80
Betty Botter bought some butter	104
Birds of a feather flock together	57
Burnie bee, burnie bee	97
Bye, baby bunting	56

C

Cackle, cackle, Mother Goose	105
Cantaloupes! Cantaloupes! What is the price?	33
Christmas is coming, the geese are getting fat	125
Cobbler, cobbler, mend my shoe	44
Cock-a-doodle-do!	24
Cock Robin got up early	47
Cocks crow in the morn to tell us to rise	29
"Come hither, little puppy dog"	100
"Come, let's to bed"	125
Cross-patch, draw the latch	57
Curly-Locks, Curly-Locks, wilt thou be mine?	48

D

Daffy-down-dilly has come to town	82
Dame Trot and her cat	96
Davy Davy Dumpling	84
Dibbity, dibbity, dibbity, doe	53
Dickory, dickory, dare	60

Page

Diddle, diddle, dumpling, my son John	68
Diddlety, diddlety, dumpty	55
Ding, dong, bell	17
Do you love me, or do you not?	125
Doctor Foster went to Gloucester	50
Donkey, donkey, old and gray	101

E

Elizabeth, Libby, Betsy and Bess	72
Elsie Marley is grown so fine	36

F

Fiddle-de-dee, fiddle-de-dee	60
"Fire! Fire!" said Mrs. Dyer	88
For every evil under the sun	124
For want of a nail, the shoe was lost	48
Friday night's dream	111
From Wibbleton to Wobbleton is fifteen miles	73

G

Georgie, Porgie, pudding and pie	104
Girls and boys, come out to play	75
Go to bed late	23
Good night, sweet repose	81
Goosey, goosey, gander	116
Great A, little a	109
Green cheese, yellow laces	61
Green gravel, green gravel	48
Gregory Griggs, Gregory Griggs	88

H

Handy dandy, riddledy ro	108
Handy Pandy, Jack-a-dandy	117
Hannah Bantry, in the pantry	40
Hark! Hark! The dogs do bark	97
Hay is for horses	124
Hearts, like doors, will open with ease	89
Hector Protector was dressed all in green	94
Here am I, little Jumping Joan	111
Here is the church, and here is the steeple	65
Here we go round the mulberry bush	62
Here's Sulky Sue	60
Hey, diddle, diddle	23
Hey diddle, dinketty, poppety, pet	41
Hey, my kitten, my kitten	116
Hickety, pickety, my black hen	53
Hickory, dickory, dock!	87
Hie to the market, Jenny come trot	61
Higglety, pigglety, pop!	57
Hob, shoe, hob	104
Hobbledy Hops, he made some tops	105
Hoddley, poddley, puddle and fogs	71
Hot boiled beans and very good butter	63
Hot cross buns, hot cross buns	80
How many days has my baby to play?	41
How many miles to Babylon?	61
Humpty Dumpty sat on a wall	111
Hush, little baby, don't say a word	71

I

I do not like thee, Doctor Fell	64
I had a little hen, the prettiest ever seen	28
I had a little hobby horse	120
I had a little husband	112
I had a little moppet	93
I had a little nut tree	97
I had a little pony	109
I had two pigeons bright and gay	52
I have seen you, little mouse	25
I love little pussy, her coat is so warm	108
I love sixpence, pretty little sixpence	109
I saw a ship a-sailing	59
I saw three ships come sailing by	34
I see the moon, and the moon sees me	74
I sing, I sing	94
If all the seas were one sea	91
If all the world were apple pie	109
If I'd as much money as I could spend	94
If wishes were horses	113
I'll tell you a story about Jack-a-Nory	29
In a cottage in Fife	21
Ipsey Wipsey spider climbing up the spout	36
It's raining, it's pouring	57

J

Jack and Jill went up the hill	39
Jack be nimble	113
Jack Sprat could eat no fat	33
"Jacky, come and give me thy fiddle"	36
Jeanie come tie my	108
Jeremiah, blow the fire	33
Jerry Hall, he is so small	61
John fought for his beloved land	101

L

Lady Queen Anne she sits in the sun	32
Ladybird, ladybird, fly away home	81
Lavender's blue, diddle, diddle	87
"Lazy Mary, will you get up?"	97
Leg over leg	116
Little Betty Blue	95
Little Blue Ben, who lives in the glen	119
Little Bo-Peep has lost her sheep	82
Little Bob Robin	115
Little Boy Blue, come blow your horn	114
Little fishes in a brook	95
"Little girl, little girl, where have you been?"	124
Little Jack Horner	119
Little Jack Pumpkin Face	121
Little King Pippin, he built a fine hall	2
Little maid, pretty maid, whither goest thou?	69
Little maiden, better tarry	81
Little Miss Muffet sat on a tuffet	98
Little miss, pretty miss	60
Little Nanny Etticoat	107
Little Poll Parrot	72
Little Polly Flinders	116
Little Robin Redbreast sat upon a rail	93
Little Robin Redbreast sat upon a tree	98
Little Sally Waters, sitting in the sun	50
Little ships must keep the shore	35
Little Tee-Wee, he went to sea	59

Little Tom Tucker	41
Little Tommy Tittlemouse	115
London Bridge is falling down	46
Lucy Locket lost her pocket	100

M

March winds and April showers	183
Mary had a little lamb	103
Mary had a pretty bird	17
Mary, Mary, quite contrary	99
Merry are the bells and merry would they ring	20
Miss One, Two and Three	33
Molly, my sister, and I fell out	29
Monday's child is fair of face	105
Moses supposes his toeses are roses	60
"Mother, may I go out to swim?"	63
Mrs. Mason bought a basin	45
Multiplication is vexation	68
My lady Wind, my lady Wind	85
My maid Mary, she minds the dairy	117

N

Needles and pins, needles and pins	40
Now what do you think of little Jack Jingle?	46

O

Of all the gay birds that e'er I did see	17
Oh, dear, what can the matter be?	64
Oh, do you know the muffin man?	104
Oh where have you been, Billy Boy, Billy Boy?	117
Oh, where, oh, where, has my little dog gone?	81
Old Farmer Giles	44
Old King Cole	42
Old Mother Goose	15
Old Mother Hubbard	102
Old Mother Shuttle	69
Old Mother Twitchett had but one eye	17
"Old woman, old woman, shall we go a-shearing?"	56
On Saturday night I lost my wife	73
Once I saw a little bird	86
One misty, moisty morning	51
One, two, buckle my shoe	63
One, two, three, four, five	40

P

Pat-a-cake, pat-a-cake, baker's man	21
Patience is a virtue	25
Pease porridge hot	36
Penny and penny	21
Peter, Peter, pumpkin eater	103
Peter White will ne'er go right	104
Pit, pat, well-a-day	49
Polly put the kettle on	121
Poor Dog Bright	69
Poor old Robinson Crusoe!	96
Pretty John Watts	62
Punch and Judy fought for a pie	40
Purple plums that hang so high	55
Puss came dancing out of a barn	48
Pussy Cat ate the dumplings	28
Pussy-Cat Mew jumped over a coal	20
Pussy-Cat, Pussy-Cat, where have you been?	37
Pussy sits beside the fire	81

		Page
Q		
Queen, Queen Caroline		56
R		
Rain on the green grass		118
Rain, rain, go away		32
Rats in the garden, catch 'em, Towser		105
Red sky at night		43
Ride a cock-horse to Banbury Cross		89
Ride away, ride away		124
Ring-a-ring o' roses		71
Rock-a-bye, baby, on the tree top		26
Round and round the rugged rock		60
Rub-a-dub-dub		47
S		
St. Swithin's Day, if thou dost rain		48
Sally go round the sun		28
See a pin and pick it up		84
See-saw, Margery Daw		92
See-saw, sacradown		73
Shoe a little horse		108
Simple Simon met a pieman		22
Sing a song of sixpence		42
Sing, sing, what shall I sing?		43
Six little mice sat down to spin		95
Sneeze on Monday, sneeze for danger		112
Snow, snow faster		22
Solomon Grundy		32
Star light, star bright		107
T		
Taffy was a Welshman		85
Tally-Ho! Tally-Ho!		23
Ten little bluebirds, perched on a pine		76
Terence McDiddler		93
The boughs do shake and the bells do ring		70
The cock's on the housetop		19
The cuckoo comes in April		124
The fair maid who, the first of May		61
The girl in the lane that couldn't speak plain		28
The greedy man is he who sits		80
The hart he loves the wild wood		22
The King of France went up the hill		65
The lion and the unicorn		25
The Man in the Moon looked out of the moon		107
The man in the wilderness said to me		72
The more rain, the more rest		50
The north wind doth blow		70
The Queen of Hearts she made some tarts		84
There was a bee		117
There was a crooked man and he went a crooked mile		33
There was a jolly miller once		89
There was a little boy went into a barn		60
There was a little girl, and she had a little curl		68
There was a man and he had naught		68
There was a man in our town		57
There was a rat, for want of stairs		41
There was an old woman and nothing she had		32
There was an old woman, and what do you think?		37
There was an old woman called Nothing-at-all		84
There was an old woman lived under a hill		18
There was an old woman of Gloucester		29
There was an old woman sat spinning		80
There was an old woman tossed up in a blanket		106
There was an old woman who lived in a shoe		66
There was an owl lived in an oak		101
There were once two cats of Kilkenny		121
There's a neat little clock		113
Thirty days hath September		72
Thirty white horses		113
This is the house that Jack built		78
This is the key of the kingdom		93
This is the way the ladies ride		53
This little man lived all alone		56
This little pig went to market		87
This old man, he played one		88
Three blind mice, see how they run!		120
Three little ghostesses		56
Three little kittens		110
Three wise men of Gotham		91
Three young rats with black felt hats		49
To make your candles last for aye		73
To market, to market, to buy a fat pig		85
Tom, Tom, the piper's son		70
Tommy Trot, a man of law		81
Tommy's tears and Mary's fears		57
Tweedledum and Tweedledee		120
Twelve pairs, hanging high		93
Twinkle, twinkle, little star		75
Two little dicky birds		24
Two little dogs sat by the fire		72
U		
Up and down the City Road		121
W		
Wash the dishes, wash the dishes		101
Wee Willie Winkie runs through the town		106
What are little boys made of?		37
What is the rhyme for porringer?		29
What's in there? Gold and money		24
"What's the news of the day?"		28
When I was a little boy, I lived by myself		44
When Jacky's a good boy		61
"Where are you going, my pretty maid?"		86
"Whistle, daughter, whistle"		45
Will you lend me your mare to ride a mile?		46
"Will you walk into my parlor?"		112
Willy boy, Willy boy, where are you going?		19
Wines and cakes for gentlemen		64
Y		
Yankee Doodle came to town		94